PRAISE FOR M

Tom Clancy fans open to a strong female lead will clamor for more.

— *DRONE*, PUBLISHERS WEEKLY

Superb! Miranda is utterly compelling!

— *BOOKLIST*, STARRED REVIEW

Miranda Chase continues to astound and charm.

— BARB M.

Escape Rating: A. Five Stars! OMG just start with *Drone* and be prepared for a fantastic binge-read!

— READING REALITY

The best military thriller I've read in a very long time. Love the female characters.

— *DRONE*, SHELDON MCARTHUR, FOUNDER OF THE MYSTERY BOOKSTORE, LA

A fabulous soaring thriller.

— *TAKE OVER AT MIDNIGHT,* MIDWEST BOOK
REVIEW

Meticulously researched, hard-hitting, and suspenseful.

— *PURE HEAT,* PUBLISHERS WEEKLY, STARRED
REVIEW

Expert technical details abound, as do realistic military missions with superb imagery that will have readers feeling as if they are right there in the midst and on the edges of their seats.

— *LIGHT UP THE NIGHT,* RT REVIEWS, 4 1/2
STARS

Buchman has catapulted his way to the top tier of my favorite authors.

— FRESH FICTION

Nonstop action that will keep readers on the edge of their seats.

— *TAKE OVER AT MIDNIGHT,* LIBRARY JOURNAL

M L. Buchman's ability to keep the reader right in the middle of the action is amazing.

— LONG AND SHORT REVIEWS

The only thing you'll ask yourself is, "When does the next one come out?"

— *WAIT UNTIL MIDNIGHT,* RT REVIEWS, 4 STARS

The first...of (a) stellar, long-running (military) romantic suspense series.

— *THE NIGHT IS MINE,* BOOKLIST, "THE 20 BEST ROMANTIC SUSPENSE NOVELS: MODERN MASTERPIECES"

I knew the books would be good, but I didn't realize how good.

— NIGHT STALKERS SERIES, KIRKUS REVIEWS

Buchman mixes adrenalin-spiking battles and brusque military jargon with a sensitive approach.

— PUBLISHERS WEEKLY

13 times "Top Pick of the Month"

IN FOR THE LONG HAUL

AN ANTARCTIC ICE FLIERS ROMANCE STORY

M. L. BUCHMAN

Buchman Bookworks

SIGN UP FOR M. L. BUCHMAN'S
NEWSLETTER TODAY

and receive:
Release News
Free Short Stories
a Free Book

Get your free book today. Do it now.
free-book.mlbuchman.com

Other works by M. L. Buchman: *(* - also in audio)*

Action-Adventure Thrillers

Dead Chef
One Chef!
Two Chef!

Miranda Chase
Drone*
Thunderbolt*
Condor*
Ghostrider*
Raider*
Chinook*
Havoc*
White Top*

Romantic Suspense

Delta Force
Target Engaged*
Heart Strike*
Wild Justice*
Midnight Trust*

Firehawks
MAIN FLIGHT
Pure Heat
Full Blaze
Hot Point*
Flash of Fire*
Wild Fire

SMOKEJUMPERS
Wildfire at Dawn*
Wildfire at Larch Creek*
Wildfire on the Skagit*

The Night Stalkers
MAIN FLIGHT
The Night Is Mine
I Own the Dawn
Wait Until Dark
Take Over at Midnight

Light Up the Night
Bring On the Dusk
By Break of Day
AND THE NAVY
Christmas at Steel Beach
Christmas at Peleliu Cove
WHITE HOUSE HOLIDAY
Daniel's Christmas*
Frank's Independence Day*
Peter's Christmas*
Zachary's Christmas*
Roy's Independence Day*
Damien's Christmas*
5E
Target of the Heart
Target Lock on Love
Target of Mine
Target of One's Own

Shadow Force: Psi
At the Slightest Sound*
At the Quietest Word*
At the Merest Glance*
At the Clearest Sensation*

White House Protection Force
Off the Leash*
On Your Mark*
In the Weeds*

Contemporary Romance

Eagle Cove
Return to Eagle Cove
Recipe for Eagle Cove
Longing for Eagle Cove
Keepsake for Eagle Cove

Henderson's Ranch
Nathan's Big Sky*
Big Sky, Loyal Heart*
Big Sky Dog Whisperer*

Other works by M. L. Buchman:

Contemporary Romance (cont)

Love Abroad
Heart of the Cotswolds: England
Path of Love: Cinque Terre, Italy

Where Dreams
Where Dreams are Born
Where Dreams Reside
Where Dreams Are of Christmas*
Where Dreams Unfold
Where Dreams Are Written

Science Fiction / Fantasy

Deities Anonymous
Cookbook from Hell: Reheated
Saviors 101

Single Titles
The Nara Reaction
Monk's Maze
the Me and Elsie Chronicles

Non-Fiction

Strategies for Success
Managing Your Inner Artist/Writer
Estate Planning for Authors*
Character Voice
Narrate and Record Your Own
Audiobook*

Short Story Series by M. L. Buchman:

Romantic Suspense

Delta Force
Th Delta Force Shooters
The Delta Force Warriors

Firehawks
The Firehawks Lookouts
The Firehawks Hotshots
The Firebirds

The Night Stalkers
The Night Stalkers 5D Stories
The Night Stalkers 5E Stories
The Night Stalkers CSAR
The Night Stalkers Wedding Stories

US Coast Guard

White House Protection Force

Contemporary Romance

Eagle Cove

Henderson's Ranch*

Where Dreams

Action-Adventure Thrillers

Dead Chef

Miranda Chase Origin Stories

Science Fiction / Fantasy

Deities Anonymous

Other
The Future Night Stalkers
Single Titles

ABOUT THIS TITLE

Clara "Sailor" Poole strode into the McMurdo Station, Antarctica heavy-equipment shop like she owned it. Finding the nerve to step into her pending wedding? Impossible.

Michel "Frenchy" Charbonneau, the self-declared Québécois hero of the ice, finally landed the great adventure: SPoT. The South Pole Traverse — the ultimate drive — from McMurdo to the South Pole. The annual thousand-mile haul to deliver two-thirds of the year's supplies to the heart of the continent.

Except Michel faces an unanticipated problem. His wedding date is fixed, but The Ice rarely cooperates with mere human plans.

1

MICHEL SPOTTED CLARA EASILY. EVEN WITH HER BACK turned and the hood of her Big Red US Antarctic Program parka up, he'd know Clara Poole anywhere— she was just that gloriously herself. The shorter figure by her side would be her best friend Priya.

They were also the only two out on the ice this morning who *weren't* in motion. The South Pole Traverse convoy was leaving McMurdo Station in about five minutes and a lot of last-minute items were being checked over.

They both shoved back their hoods for the warm spring weather. Clara's black hair fluttered about her shoulders. So lovely to play with—it was one of his hundred or so most favorite things about her.

Michel wasn't quite sure why Priya was here but he suspected that it was important, if only he could figure it out.

He heard them talking as he came up from behind.

Clara's voice was deep and New England curt, "You better stay my best friend even after we leave The Ice. If you don't, I'll die."

Priya laughed. "I didn't think anything could kill a Gloucesterwoman. Isn't that what you told me the first time we met?"

"I lied. With the wedding coming, I'm rattled down to my boots."

"How is it that you're marrying a man with a girl's name?" Priya began singing the inevitable Beatles' song, *Michelle, my belle.*

"He's Québécois French, he can't help it." Clara crossed her hands over her chest. "I think my heart is going to explode."

"Eww! Don't get any on me." Priya shuffled away across the hard-packed snow.

Clara snagged her by the loose end of her scarf and hauled her back to which Priya made a show of choking and gasping desperately, drawing everyone's attention.

Michel felt Clara's shiver as he wrapped his arms around her from behind.

It was already up in the twenties though it was still early October. Yet despite the warm day, she shivered even as she leaned back into him. She knew him as easily as he knew her. Their connection was without question. Priya always accused them of being a "penguin couple," able to find each other without fail in a million-bird colony.

It *definitely* wasn't the cold. Clara and Priya were not alone in easing their heavy winter clothes. All of the winterovers and many of the summerfolk here for their "life's great adventure" at MacTown were walking around with their parkas open and hoods thrown back like it was time to hit the water slides at Village Vacances Valcartier back in Québec.

A spring this warm said they could have whole record-breaking days above freezing by Christmas at McMurdo Station. Priya, being a marine biologist, was already freaking out about shifting food vectors and the potential for massive die-offs. Though she covered that with a sharp sense of humor.

For being a "beaker"—an Antarctic scientist—she was actually a lot of fun.

Clara turned inside the curve of his arms, snuggled inside his open parka, and buried her face against his shoulder. He held her tight but addressed Priya.

"How's the maid of honor today?"

"How's the chief lummox?"

"I'm not a lemming," he purposely misunderstood her.

"Sure you are, you're rushing out onto the sea." She waved her hand to indicate the vast sweep the Antarctic continent. "Just warning you. You hurt my friend, I'm going to stuff you down a crevasse."

Clara shivered again, which wasn't like her at all.

He rested his cheek against her temple.

"Hey, Sailor."

"Hey, Jean Pierre."

Since the day they'd met, she'd never called him by the same name twice—ever. She'd also had never used his real name, Michel Charbonneau, or his nickname of Frenchy.

Maybe it really was pre-wedding nerves rather than the cold making her shiver. He glanced at Priya again. Moral support. Yeah, that fit.

The weather *was* an issue but not a cold one.

The sun had first risen two months ago.

After tonight, when it dipped below the horizon ever so briefly, it wouldn't set again for four months.

But the reason Clara was shivering loomed in front of them: a convoy of huge tractors.

The SPoT convoy was departing McMurdo in minutes. And he was one of the drivers.

A third of the fuel and supplies for the South Pole Station were flown in from McMurdo by a series of seventy-six flights. The LC-130 Skibirds of the New York Air National Guard 109th Airlift Wing would start flitting south in a few weeks when the South Pole was warm enough that the plane engines didn't freeze on landing.

But now was the time for the land-crawling SPoT to get a move on. The tractor convoy delivered the remaining two-thirds of the supplies by dragging them over the ice and snow of the one thousand-and-thirty-five-mile McMurdo-South Pole Highway, more commonly known as the South Pole Traverse—SPoT. There was time for three trips a season, as long as they hustled.

"How *did* I fall in love with a man named like a girl?" Clara sounded a little more like herself. It was also as close as she ever came to using his real name.

"Because you had the good sense to fall for the dashing Québécois hero of Antarctica." He kissed her on the ear.

"Tell me how falling for a Frenchman makes any sense. No, don't." She kept her head on his shoulder. "You'll somehow make it sound wicked sensible, like when you proposed."

"I thought you proposed to me. Either way, I am pretty irresistible. I have that on the best authority."

"I should never have mentioned that." She hugged him harder inside his Big Red which had cocooned around them.

"Don't worry, I'll be back in plenty of time for the wedding."

"You better be." She thumped a fist against his ribs.

He caught her hand before she could get serious about it, because Clara was strong. He pinned it over his heart. "I'm wearing your sweater."

"You'd better. I took a mad risk making that for

you." She'd told him there was a knitters' myth—she called it a truth—that when you spent all of the effort to knit a sweater for a boyfriend, that would invariably end the relationship. She'd done it anyway because it was Clara who never quite followed the rules.

That he'd misinterpreted the elaborate colorwork of the beautiful Fair Isle knit gift as a proposal had earned him one of her electric smiles and a splendid tussle as she peeled him back out of it. Saying "yes" when he'd thought it was a proposal was so obvious that he hadn't hesitated. Something that had made *him* shiver a time or two since. How had it been so ridiculously easy to agree to marry a woman including that death-do-us-part bit?

Right now, she was the one who was all nerves— which actually made him feel a little calmer. They were weird that way and it often made them laugh. Not today.

"Three weeks out, a five-day layover, and three weeks back. We're good for the wedding with a week to spare." The window between the first and second traverse was very narrow, but he didn't point that out. For the next four months, he'd be spending all but turn-around weeks driving back and forth across half the continent.

She kept her face buried against his shoulder.

"Maybe you two should just elope," Priya chimed in.

"Great idea. Let's go." Michel spun Clara free of his

arms and grabbed her hand because, at this rate, he'd never be able to let go of her. Her hugs should come with a license. Actually they did, a marriage license. Now he was the one feeling all the nerves.

To mask them, he took one step as if to lead off.

"Wait, where are we eloping to?"

Clara gave him the laugh he wanted.

"The Kiwis?" Priya suggested.

"I don't know. Scott Base is only three kilometers away. Not much of an elopement. You know us Québécois heroes, if we do something, we do it with style. What do you say, my love, do we wait it out or throw ourselves on our New Zealand compatriots?"

Clara sighed. "We wait."

In eight weeks, her South Carolina grandparents would be visiting her parents in Gloucester. Her big brother and little sister had agreed to come up from New York and Washington, DC. Michel's parents and brother were driving down from Québec so that the two families could finally meet. And then they were all going to be together to video conference in for the "big wedding."

A wedding on The Ice would also be an excuse for a grand party on their end as well. Any excuse for a party was embraced here, but this one was going to be all out of proportion with McMurdo humming at summerfolk volumes and a wedding to celebrate.

Everything was all arranged. Except Clara would be here doing her job at McMurdo while Michel drove a tractor across a thousand miles of ice to the South Pole and back.

The first tractor engine roared to life.

"That's my cue to kiss the woman I love—"

"—and then leave her standing flatfooted on the snow." Priya jumped in.

"*Mais oui!*" Then he kissed Clara hard and whispered seriously in her ear. "I'll be careful, and safe, and back before you know it, Sailor. I love you more permanently than all the ice in the world," Clara's catchphrase after they'd become engaged. You couldn't be in Antarctica and not firmly believe in global warming.

Rico, the Manager of Traverse Operations, yelled his name and he turned for his tractor.

He glanced back to see Priya slip an arm around Clara's waist. She spoke loudly enough for Michel to easily hear her despite the rumbling tractors, "That man did *not* just whisper a sweet nothing in your ear."

"He absolutely did."

He bent down to check his boot laces at the edge of hearing, because she wasn't hurting his ego at all.

"Damn it! One good man on the planet and you get him. How is that even possible?"

"Well, I have you for a best friend, so I must be doing something right."

"Which means, since you got the man, I must be doing everything wrong. So having *you* as a bestie just makes me a sad sack."

"It does," Michel pushed to his feet and called back.

Priya flicked him the finger and laughed, but Clara just looked sad.

He returned Priya's salute, but he was out of time to do anything about the latter.

2

MICHEL CLIMBED UP INTO HIS CHALLENGER MT865 AND
fired off the big diesel engine with a throaty roar that
shook the very air. The big agricultural tractor, with
massive treads like a tank instead of wheels, had been
modified for the cold with sealed engine
compartments, several engine heaters, and satellite
radios which would allow them to communicate from
out on the ice.

Rico lurched the lead snowcat into motion. It had a
long front boom reaching forward. At its end dangled a
ground-penetrating radar for detecting new crevasses
so that no one drove into one.

There were eight tractors this trip. Six of them
dragged massive thirty-foot wide, sixty-foot long sleds.
On each of these was strapped eight, three-thousand-
gallon fuel bladders for delivery to the South Pole
Station. Eighty tons of fuel encapsulated in massive

black-rubber beans, each seven-and-a-half feet wide, thirty-long, and filled until they rose a yard high.

Another sled carried several containers' worth of cargo, supplies too big or heavy to be easily flown to the pole.

And the last tractor, Michel's, dragged their living-quarters modules: repair shop, bunkhouse, and the combined kitchen, dining, and living room. Aside from a few days at the South Pole, for the next two months, it would be just the nine of them: one driver in the lead snowcat and eight in the tractors.

He was late enough to the line, that he was on the move the moment his engine was up to temperature. The line stretched out slowly as they moved down from the station onto the ice. McMurdo perched on Ross Island, the farthest south land accessible by ship —very briefly each year—and they'd be driving across the ice shelf for the first six hundred miles.

By the time he thought to turn and wave, the big living modules blocked all visibility behind. Yet another reason he was last in line.

He waved anyway, but knew it was lame.

He remembered clearly the first time he'd met Clara, perhaps because it had been her first day at McMurdo just a year ago. She'd walked into the heavy equipment shed and undone her Big Red parka like an old hand, not that it was much warmer inside than outside.

The boss had said they were expecting someone

new on the next flight, but that's all he'd said. The FINGY—Fucking New Guy—was a FIN...GAL.

He'd been with the guys, grouped around a fire truck; the fire department was the single biggest team at the US stations of McMurdo and the South Pole. The entire cab—seats and all—had been tipped up and forward out of the way, the whole assembly pivoting at the front bumper. Beneath it, the big diesel engine lay exposed on the chassis.

She'd walked into the circle to stare down at the engine with the rest of them as if she'd always been part of their circle. Only because he'd been facing her had he seen the brief hesitation in her step before she did so. Nerves, but nerves of steel as it was the only sign she gave.

Clara always walked with the rolling gait of a captain striding the deck of her ship. Only later did he find out she'd come by it honestly from years of working on her family's fishing boats out of Gloucester, Massachusetts.

"What's it doing?" Clara's idea of a warm greeting.

"It *iz* what she *iz no* doing," Michel had teased her, stressing his French.

"Not working, Claude." She gave the made-up name a heavy French pronunciation.

"Got it in one, Sailor." His tag of Sailor had stuck, which still tickled him no end.

"Symptoms, Henri?" The name *du jour* thing already had the guys laughing with her—*at* him.

"Broken," he continued with determined unhelpfulness. This was too much fun.

She'd laughed in his face. Not nasty, he'd decided, just enjoying herself.

"Won't start," the crew boss had made it clear who was in charge by his tone. "It'll crank, but no fire."

"Meter?" She'd taken the boss' folded arms not as a challenge, but as if he was waiting for her to do her stuff.

Michel had pointed to the nearby tool case. She scanned the shop with a single sweep before turning to fetch a meter. The shop here was pro caliber. There was no sending out the trickier repairs when the next nearest shop was five hours away in Christchurch, New Zealand—by jet. They did it all here and had the equipment to build almost any part they didn't stock.

It had taken her two minutes to ring out the wires —finding the only one that didn't peep when she put the meter's test leads on either end—and find the culprit that had eluded them for the last thirty minutes.

Then she must have noticed their frustrated expressions. He was feeling some of that himself. She had somehow reached into the massive wire harnesses and found the one fault.

"When there wasn't any fishing, I worked as a mechanic for the Gloucester Fire Department. Took care of their engines." That chilled everyone out, but she'd looked puzzled by the pattern of damage once she found the fractured component.

"Freeze-heat cycle," Michel had explained. "Minus fifty or sixty, then you fire off the engine. The temperature swing will stress crack just about anything."

And in some way that he still didn't understand, his giving her a straight answer when it mattered had started them off on exactly the right foot.

Women were still low density creatures on The Ice, maybe a quarter of the beakers but rarely crossing ten percent in the support teams. Just stepping on the continent upped any woman's hotness by at least a factor of two. That hadn't touched Clara. She couldn't look any other way being who she was—not that she needed the boost.

Dammit! He really should have remembered to wave goodbye once he was in the cab.

The SPoT team departure was mostly a non-event at McMurdo. The same crew that had done most of the loading was also doing the driving. Nine people leaving McMurdo's throng, which was almost at its fifteen-hundred-person summer peak, was hardly noteworthy. Small expeditions left almost every day for one summer science camp or another.

And while the SPoT team was driving across the polar ice cap, someone had to keep the home fires from burning. It was Clara's job to stay behind this summer.

He definitely should have waved.

Baptême! He was *un idiot!* He had something far better.

He leaned on the horn, releasing a loud blast. Off to the sides, he could see people twisting around to look. Not so anonymous today.

When he released the horn, he could hear others in the convoy, blasting theirs. He hit his again.

There was a bright ping from his pager—the only reliable way to send short messages away from base.

He stopped honking to pull it out.

A smiley from Clara. He'd done good.

He hit the horn again.

3

WHEN MICHEL HAD PICTURED HIS LIFE IN ANTARCTICA, before arriving, he'd never thought it would be spent as one of the city mice. Most of the McMurdoans never ranged more than walking distance from the largest town on the entire continent. As a fuelie and truck driver, he often drove out onto the ice shelf to build and service the ice runways, but that was still only a matter of a few kilometers from MacTown.

Last year he'd been told he'd be on the next year's SPoT crew if he wanted to stay overwinter. A Challenger MT865 tractor couldn't have dragged him away. He'd turned down a chance for a late summer break in Christchurch, New Zealand. There was always a chance of bad weather closing The Ice early and he wasn't going to risk getting stuck ashore.

He knew he'd made the right choice when Clara

had strolled into the machine shop the next day as if she already owned the place.

Her competence was what he'd come to expect from the others who'd made the grade to get to The Ice. Her understated confidence had been captivating. And her Gloucester accent had done him in—the New England-rough just fit her so perfectly.

And now that he finally had his place on the SPoT and his dream of getting out of MacTown was coming true? He was missing Clara. It had taken months into winter lockdown before she'd let him slide into her bed, but in hindsight he could see that she'd slid right under his guard that first day.

He was the last to jostle slowly over the transition from Ross Island onto the Ross Ice Shelf. Looking back, his rearview mirror still showed nothing except for the living-quarters module he was dragging along, but he couldn't stop looking. He knew she'd still be there watching him drive out of sight.

That had been the unexpected treat, the truffle-sweet woman inside that hard-candy shell.

They drove out of McMurdo, out onto the Ross Ice Shelf, and swung wide around Discovery Hut where Scott had started his ill-fated expedition to the South Pole.

"Please don't let that be a portent of what's to come."

Nobody answered, of course. For the entire drive, he'd be alone in a glass box, driving a tractor at five miles an hour for ten to twelve hours a day. There would be breaks for meals, refueling, and sleeping, but the main thing to look forward to was utter monotony —or so he'd been told.

"Still with us, Frenchy?" His nickname to everyone except Clara. He realized that this call on the radio hadn't been the first.

"Depends, is today Thursday?"

"Monday."

"Oh, *non monsieur*. Ne-*ver* on a Monday."

"He's already zoning out in the first five miles."

"Buckle down, Frenchy. We've got a long road ahead."

And the banter continued. He did his part to keep it moving. But it soon faded away, and it was once again him, alone in a glass box, driving over the great expanse of white ice.

His first winter on The Ice, his life had slowed down, just as everyone's did through the long months of darkness and isolation. The Second Winter had spun up like his life was out of control.

Even in the very beginning Clara Poole hadn't just been some pleasant distraction. A woman who understood engines better than he did was to be admired. A woman who knew them *so* much better was a little humbling. He recognized mastery when he saw it. So, he'd made sure that he was always there when she needed an extra hand just so that he could learn.

The payoff of Clara herself...well, he had no reference for that in his life.

He'd grown up chasing slim French girls, so perfectly coy, around the Les Galeries de la Capitale shopping mall. A brash, ballbuster of a Gloucesterwoman wasn't the sort of woman he'd ever met before.

Christ, would he have been confident enough to roll into an unknown machine shop and just jump in the way she had? A Québécois might have done it with bravado to take control, she'd done it with blinding skill.

And... *Baptême!*

He yanked back on the speed control and the engine throttle. He'd almost climbed right up the back of the supply sled being dragged by the tractor in front of him. Thankfully, even skidding across the ice, the big loads stopped quickly. But it was a sure bet that the kitchen cupboards he was hauling were going to be a real jumble.

He checked the clock. Six hours, they'd come thirty miles.

Even *thinking* about that woman wiped out big chunks of time.

He tried looking back, but *again* all he saw were the living-quarter modules. Any hint of McMurdo was long gone. It was just their machines—and the vast white.

To his left was a great expanse of flat nothing and

to his right more flat, abutting the white land climbing up until it hit the blue sky. There was no way to tell if it was a two-hundred-foot hummock just a few soccer fields away, or a line of mountains parked along the horizon. Either way, white.

Ahead, the tractors weren't moving.

Only thirty miles out. That's when he knew why they'd stopped. They were in the McMurdo Shear Zone where the McMurdo and Ross ice shelves ground against each other, deciding who got to go which way around Ross Island while shoving ice into the sea. That the convoy had come to a full stop wasn't a particularly bad sign.

The road crew had already been out this way weeks ago, making sure the way through the Shear Zone was clear. But ice was never still. Even at the South Pole, near the center of the continent, the ice cap slipped along at ten meters a year. Out here it was much more lively—a hundred times faster, roughly a kilometer a year.

Up in the lead, Rico in the snowcat would be out prowling around with his radar, checking for any new crevasses that might have formed. Hopefully, any new ones would be small enough to crawl over but some could be big enough that they'd need a route around. It all had to be preplanned because one thing that a Challenger MT865 treaded tractor towing an eighty-ton sled could *not* do was back up.

He toyed with several riffs on, "He's so dumb that

he thinks reverse is a gear on a SPoT tractor." But he hadn't come up with a good one by the time the "All clear" was given and they could start edging ahead.

He should have paged Clara while he was waiting, she was really good at things like that. She and Priya often worked out two-person verbal traps for their friends to fall into—he'd certainly been their victim often enough.

Michel reached for his two-way radio, but it wasn't going to reach McMurdo, now thirty miles over the horizon. Except for pager pings and spendy satellite calls, they were already well and surely cut off from the world—eight tractors alone on an endless desert of ice.

Cut off from Clara, too.

It was crazy, but the latter was the one that felt far more burdensome.

What had she done to him?

4

THE PROBLEM DIDN'T GET ANY BETTER OF THE NEXT TEN days. For six hundred miles past the McMurdo Shear Zone he had nothing else to think about.

Crossing the vast flat of the Ross Ice Shelf offered no distractions. There were only so many hours you could spend envisioning the fuel flow through the system. He wasn't a big fan of audiobooks, so it was mostly just watching the world go by.

It was twenty degrees outside, but the sun shone twenty-four hours a day. He'd been told to bring shorts and a t-shirt for the drive, which he'd assumed was a prank on the FINGY—despite a year on The Ice, he'd become the fucking new guy all over again when he joined the SPoT convoy. In fact, he was the only new driver on the team this year.

But the shorts hadn't been a joke and he was glad that he'd tucked them out of sight deep in his bag.

They were headed to the South Pole, all wearing shorts and t-shirts, sitting in their cabs, and slathered in sunscreen with the door open. Between the engines and the sun, the heat, not the cold, was the problem.

Once he fell into the rhythm of the day, he became more and more aware of how Clara had changed him.

He wondered what she was up to now. Probably servicing all of the pumps on the long fuel lines that stretched across the ice to the McMurdo runways. Tens of thousands of gallons would be transported out to the smaller planes exhausted by their crossing from New Zealand. Hundreds of thousands would be pumped into the Air National Guard planes as they ferried back and forth to the South Pole. During the brief fall-season melt out, an icebreaker-escorted fuel ship would offload five million gallons to restock the McMurdo tank farm.

Since when did he spend time wondering about a woman?

Since he'd fallen in love with a Yankee.

Being around her was like being addicted to a drug. He was a pretty mellow guy, but she never settled to rest. And he'd been swept up in it.

Now, he was quite content to just roll along, fifty meters behind the next nearest sled, one hand on the wheel, the other tapping along to the playlist his little brother kept pumped up for him. Clara would be worrying about the engine, or listening to an audiobook about the Antarctic explorers, or taking

French lessons. Who knew what all the woman did, but she somehow filled every spare moment.

Not that she never relaxed, but she relaxed just as hard as she worked.

Their first movie night together had included fifteen tiny bowls of everything from M&Ms and licorice bits to trail mix, dried apple slices, candied ginger, and other scrounged treats. She'd set up a film fest of "mechanic's" movies. They'd slouched together and nibbled their way through: *The Flight of the Phoenix* (the original not the remake), *Days of Thunder* (for Duvall, not Tom Cruise, she was very clear about that though he'd enjoyed watching Nicole Kidman himself), *Gone in 60 Seconds* (Duvall again but he shouldn't be jealous), and *Apollo 13*. They'd fallen asleep before the old submarine movie *Run Silent Run Deep*.

Out here on the Ross Ice Shelf it felt as if he was taking his first breath since meeting Clara.

The thought made him feel guilty.

He was engaged to Clara Poole. He *loved* Clara Poole. There was no question that he'd ever meet another woman like her, but who was he becoming?

5

HALFWAY ACROSS THE ICE SHELF, THEY LOST THE LAST sight of any land. Three hundred miles behind them, the twelve-thousand-foot volcanic cone of Mt. Erebus finally faded into the horizon. No land within a hundred miles in any direction. They were in the middle of the ocean which lay beneath a thousand feet of ice.

They made good time over the relatively flat ice, sometimes running as high as seventy miles a day. If they kept that up, they'd make the round trip too fast and he'd be leaving McMurdo for the second SPoT run *before* the wedding. *Baptême,* but The Ice made everything complicated—even a good Québécois religious curse didn't cover the depth of that.

The logistics of everything here was just that crazy. By the time they delivered a gallon of fuel to the South Pole and it was actually burned, it would cost forty dollars US—thirty-nine of that would be transport and storage.

At night, when the sun was a little closer to the horizon than at midday, they stopped the tractors and climbed down from the cabs. It was too dangerous to wander far, they stayed within thirty or forty feet of the traverse path. To either side lay the unsurveyed nothingness. Even a tiny crevasse could swallow a man with no one the wiser, no more than a small hole in the snow where he'd disappeared. Whether the crevasse opened ten feet deep—or all the way down to the ocean's surface—the end result would probably be the same.

He really needed to stop finding metaphors of the ice conditions to his mental ones—like wondering just how deep a hole had his heart already fallen down.

In the kitchen, they took turns cooking. The next day's cooks would prowl through the ambient temperature food locker deciding what they were going to bring inside to thaw for tomorrow.

One of the hot topics was the upcoming wedding. All guys on the convoy this year, so the talk kept veering toward the "wedding night."

"There won't be one, not until the sun sets." That had sidetracked them from that topic—for almost five minutes.

He couldn't seem to get away from it.

Nine days out on the traverse, Rico waved for him to join in an after-dinner walk. "Come on, Frenchy. We start the climb tomorrow. I want to doublecheck everything."

It was a lame excuse, as they'd already done the daily post-drive full inspections of their rigs. The safety checks weren't optional when the nearest help was now five hundred miles away in every direction. Even the next emptiest place on Earth, the center of the Greenland ice cap, was only three hundred miles from either coast. By comparison, central Siberia was a hotbed of civilization. Here it was only snow, ice, and their pinprick of a convoy.

As soon as they'd stopped for the day, they'd patrolled the treads with a steel breaker bar, knocking loose any snow and ice buildup in the wheels that drove the treads. Left overnight, it could turn steel-hard and damage the running gear. Visual inspections, check the oil, the hydraulic levels, possible ice in the air cleaner...they went through it all every night.

"What are you sitting on, Frenchy?" Rico asked as they began working their way forward along the convoy.

"Other than my ass?"

Rico raised a baseball bat and whacked it against the drive wheel for the tractor's big rubber tread. It offered the right sort of clank in response. Michel's own ear had quickly learned how to accurately read the gear's condition with the tone of that clank. Dull thud, there was hidden ice in there. Any rattle, it was time to check for any loose hardware. That clank with just a bit of a ring to it? Sweet.

Rumor said Rico was as old as the ice. One story told how they'd found him frozen in the ice when they built McMurdo. Another that he'd been left behind by the Scott Expedition in 1912 and had built all of McMurdo himself while waiting for the Americans to come back in 1956.

It was also clear that Michel was going to be Rico's next target with that bat, so he did his best to answer the question straight.

"I guess I'm getting more time to think than is good for me." He wasn't exactly *doubting* Clara. He was more doubting her sanity in wanting to marry him. He'd never struck himself as the marrying kind. Shack up with some sexy *artiste*? Sure. Monogamous? No problem, he'd always been that sort for as long as anything lasted. But marriage? His record longest relationship had been his eight months with Clara.

Rico was silent as they poked and prodded their way around the big cargo sled. In fact, he'd didn't speak again until they were checking the ground-penetrating radar on the lead snowcat.

"Frenchy, do yourself a favor."

"If I gotta do one, might as well be for myself, right?"

"Right. Stop thinking so much. My wife said she knew from the first day that we would be married. I was maybe ten, she was nine when we met."

Michel hadn't even heard about Rico being married.

"Married to her was the best twenty years of my life until she died too young." He was silent most of the way back to the living quarters.

"So what's the favor?"

Rico's baseball bat slapped against his butt. "You so dense that you need me to spell it out? Fine. This thing with Clara?"

"Yeah."

"You fuck it up, I'm gonna shove you down a crevasse, an ocean-deep one. Nobody will ever find your body."

He stepped inside and left Michel standing out in the cold sun.

6

MICHEL SUPPOSED THAT THE BRUTALITY OF THE NEXT DAY was only appropriate.

The climb from the Ross Ice Shelf through the Transantarctic Mountains—with a few inevitable lame jokes about the T&A mountains—to the polar plateau was a steep one up the rolled front of the glacier which fed the shelf. Depending on how the ice shelf was floating, they started at a hundred feet or so above sea level. By tonight, they'd be at nine thousand feet atop the polar plateau.

While the tractors were robust enough to haul their loads over rough terrain, the steep climb was too much, so they had to hook up and haul loads in tandem, making two trips. Hooking and unhooking all the sleds and tractors was going to be the most exposed work of the entire trip.

That was the first problem. The air sliding down off

the polar plateau was only marginally warmed by the sun, little above minus seventy Fahrenheit, even this late in the spring. And the long slope meant that the cold, dense air was blasting downslope which raised a near whiteout of blowing ice and snow. Straight overhead, the world was blue sky. Looking ahead, it was hard to see the next tractor, never mind the next flag.

Each year, a team ran the route prior to the traverse convoy's passage, staking a flag every quarter mile for the entire length. Every two to three years, the entire route was resurveyed due to the movement of the ice. GPS was only so useful when some sections of the surveyed-safe route moved multiple kilometers in a year and others didn't move much at all. It was the flags that marked the safe passage—hopefully.

After the long double-haul up onto the polar plateau, everything else took twice as much effort as well. Even sitting still as they drove across five hundred more miles of flat nothingness was exhausting. The cold was so intense now, that it punched hard against the cabin heater's limits. The passage from the tractor cab to their living quarters was "mad cold" as Clara would say.

When Michel decided that he envied the engines —their enclosure modifications ran them as if they were in just minus twenty degree weather, not minus seventy—he knew he was losing it. It was too cold up here to even crack a window, yet the sun continued to cook them on one side while they chilled on the other in their little glass cubes atop the powerful machines.

From the top of the climb southwards, the tractors began having problems. Not mechanical problems; power problems. Hauling eighty tons of fuel with each tractor at sea level made the Challengers seem indomitable. Doing the same thing at nine thousand feet, up atop the plateau of the polar ice cap made them gasp and wheeze at every imperfection in the SPoT road.

The road, *Baptême!* The path packed by last year's traverse and then carved up by the constantly blown snow of the long winter was wicked harsh (thanks, Clara). It rarely snowed here, but the drifting never, ever stopped. Driving at speed across the surface, the tractor would abruptly tilt and groan as it struggled over some new drift.

A thousand miles at a brisk walk. Very brisk at these temperatures. Without enough air. His body refused to adapt quickly to the high elevation. Even the regulars were pretty subdued those first nights high on the ice cap.

The rest of the passage passed in a blur. A four-hundred-mile crawl over the plateau.

With fifty miles to go, which should have been an easy day's haul, they plunged into hell. Hearing about "Sastrugi National Park" and experiencing it were too very different things.

"Just start the morning by putting all your crap on

the floor, it'll end up there anyway. And buckle your damn seatbelt," Rico wasn't the only one to warn him.

Sastrugi weren't piled-up snow drifts that the plow on the lead tractor could flatten out. It was hard ice that had been deeply wind-carved by the fierce winds that plagued the South Pole. And in the so-called National Park the carved ridges were three meters high. Despite the deep seat cushions and springs, Michel knew he'd be black and blue after the first half hour. With full loads, they were beaten and battered for two full days, as they ground over the hard ice dragging their big sleds.

No one slept well the night they spent in the sastrugi, there'd simply been no way to level the living quarters. The constant feeling of falling out of the tilted bunks gave everyone nightmares.

At noon the next day, they emerged from Sastrugi Hell and plunged into the Swamp. With the beacon of the bright blue station looking like a mirage twenty miles away, it was hard to pay attention to the ice road.

And nowhere could it be more critical. It was a curious region with almost no wind at all. Rather than carved hell, the snow stayed light and fluffy here in broad drifts. Straying from the road, well packed by prior years of passage, was just asking to get high-centered and deeply stuck. Then an elaborate game of unhooking one or two of the other tractors to haul out the stuck tractor and sled, without swamping those tractors in turn, had filled the stories around the dinner table for several nights.

Michel made sure that he stuck right on the tread marks of the machine in front of him the whole way across.

The passage, being the first full traverse of the year, had taken twenty-seven days instead of the more typical twenty-one. They were still on schedule for him to be back in time for the wedding—barely.

For four weeks he'd seen no one new and spoken only to the SPoT crew. Other than a few pager-emails with Clara, he'd had no contact with the outside world. Their tiny group had bonded, pulled tight by the shared hardship and isolation.

7

THEIR ARRIVAL AT SOUTH POLE STATION WAS ACTUALLY a little terrifying.

They were swarmed on their arrival. It was finally warm enough, only minus fifty-three Fahrenheit, for the planes to fly safely, but a storm up at McMurdo had delayed them. The SPoT convoy were the first visitors in over eight months. The forty-one overwinters mobbed them.

For them, the SPoT team were the first new faces of the year and were a welcome relief. Like two old whaling ships meeting for the first time in a multi-year voyage, there was an overwhelming social explosion.

There was also a lot of work.

The cargo sled was unloaded.

The fuel bladders were hooked up to temporary tanks and pumped dry. The team chased the dregs of fuel out of the flaccid rubber bladders with push brooms, salvaging every gallon possible from the hard rubber going stiff with the cold. Only three bladders of the forty-eight they'd dragged south were left full, nine thousand gallons to fuel their return trip.

Nothing was thrown out at the Pole, the Antarctic Treaty prohibited it. A lot of the crap went out on the planes, but again, the too big and too awkward were theirs to haul back. A decommissioned building was loaded onto the cargo sled along with numerous pallets of recycling, costing them another crucial day.

And through the whole six-day unload and load operation, it seemed to Michel that he was being pulled a hundred different ways.

Work on the tractors.

Grab a shower. Even limited to two minutes due to fuel costs, it was a *huge* luxury after three weeks of sponge baths. Laundry was another major plus.

Every meal was spent surrounded by the overwinters eager for new stories. That pressure eased a little when the first plane of the season finally made it in—delivering a load of scientists, support staff, and fresh fruit and veggies which he missed so much it was hard to believe it had only been three weeks. At McMurdo, they were five months without freshies. How they made it the nearly nine months at the South Pole taught him that his tentative idea to overwinter at the South Pole someday should probably stay tentative.

One of the team mentioned his upcoming Ice

Wedding. That made him the center of even more attention. Weddings on The Ice were one of the latest offerings by tour companies. But to have two of "their own" get married on Antarctica was turning out to be a big deal.

The whole week at the South Pole was a dizzying whirlwind that didn't give him time to think.

The only time he felt half himself were the two brief calls he'd managed with Clara. Communications satellite coverage—the only kind there was here—was spotty at the South Pole and there was no bandwidth for video calls. But both times they'd managed to talk and laugh a little. Long enough to get past the "brave front" they each were keeping up for the other.

"Separation makes the heart grow fonder?" she'd asked softly at the end of the second conversation. He'd barely managed to nod before the connection failed. Realizing she couldn't have seen his nod, he paged back, "It does."

Once more in his rig at the end of the convoy, he turned north. From here, every direction was north. McMurdo drew at him like a compass, but also pushed back against his nerves like the wrong end of a magnet.

He leaned on the horn when a few of the workers who were out to service another Skibird delivery flight waved.

But his heart wasn't in it.

The peace of The Ice wrapped around him long before the station was out of sight. Even when the

Number Three tractor wandered into The Swamp and Number Four almost followed it in, he didn't mind—except for the eight hours it took to haul the sleds and tractors back onto the trail.

Mostly it was just him and his tractor.

He was okay with that. This he understood.

His own message still on his pager's screen to Clara's question of whether separation made the heart grow fonder—"It does."—not so much.

8

It wasn't Sastrugi National Park that got them.
That merely battered them body and soul. Getting
seasick at nine thousand feet was a little bizarre, but
the constant climb and descent over the uneven ice-
carved field had him wishing for a stable horizon long
before they reached it. Two separate breakdowns
happened due to the shaking. It cost them a day he no
longer had to spare.

It wasn't the Polar Plateau that got them. They
crossed that vast expanse with as few events as they
had on the outbound journey—nothing that took over
a few hours to fix.

It wasn't even a crevasse.

It was "Sonic" Borowski's heart. The big Pole didn't
speak much, but he had a laugh that blasted into being
like a sonic boom at the strangest moments. You

couldn't *not* laugh in response when Sonic launched one.

He was driving the cargo tractor directly ahead of Michel when he abruptly veered aside.

Michel barely resisted the urge to follow him as he had for over thirty days of driving.

Sonic's tractor made it past a hundred meters off the road before it climbed an ice drift—only under one side. It tilted in slow motion until it tumbled onto its side. The treads continued spinning as the tractor lay there.

"Man down!" he shouted over the radio. Then he shoved open his cabin door, jumped down to the ice, and cursed. It was minus sixty-five and blowing hard. It felt as if he was having a full-body acupuncture by ice crystals. He climbed back into his cab, shrugged into his parka, and grabbed his heavy gloves before jumping down again.

First on the scene, he avoided the spinning treads to reach the cabin door. Through the glass he could see Sonic hanging lax in his seat harness. It was about the scariest thing he'd ever seen.

He crawled in and killed the engine, stopping the treads, and hopefully before there was any damage to the engine. It was hard not to step on all the detritus that had built up over five weeks in a confined space and now been dumped onto the side window and ceiling. Soda cans, a couple novels, water bottles, a pair of socks and a loner in another color, a whole collection of small boxes—Sonic must have a major sweet tooth for Raisinets.

He still had a pulse, but that was all Michel was qualified to test. That and the man's breath was clear in the cold air. He squatted with Sonic's head supported in his lap until the other guys showed up.

Rico led half the team to haul Sonic to the living quarters. He shouted instructions as he moved off. "Frenchy, get a couple of the guys to right this tractor. Then figure out if it's drivable."

It took them an hour in the bitter cold. First they had to get the tractor with the snowplow unhooked from its sled, then cut away the ice dune that had tipped Sonic's tractor. Two more tractors with lines rigged, tipped the tractor upright.

Risking the skin on his fingers, he pulled the injectors and cranked the engine with the power off. Only a little oil squirted out the holes—a good sign that not too much oil had leaked into the cylinders while running inverted.

He slid the injectors back in, and ran the block and sump heaters for twenty minutes before he tried cranking it over. The cloud of white smoke out the stack was so thick that the wind couldn't quite rip it away. But in under a minute, the smoke was already tapering off and—he nearly froze his ear to the chassis to check—there was no engine knock that he could detect.

The cab was battered and far from airtight, but it was intact.

They reattached the cargo sled and, using all three tractors, managed to tow it back onto the track.

The outside team conferred quickly. "If Sonic can't drive…" "…we can put his tractor on one of the empty sleds." "Yeah, then we double up some of the empty fuel sleds to free up a tractor for the cargo module."

Michel made a point of high-fiving the whole team for having it down. It would mean moving slower, probably a half day to rejigger the loads and then at *least* an extra day of driving.

He was going to miss his own goddamn wedding. Clara was going to lambast him—because their families would be scattering back to the winds the next day. And family was at the core of who Clara was.

As they hustled over to the living-quarters module, Michel had another thought that almost took his knees out from under him.

It was the first time he'd thought about the crevasses. They were nearing the head of the glacier, where it bent and folded for the nine-thousand-foot descent to form the Ross Ice Shelf, and he'd been running around on the surface like it was a hockey rink.

Tabarnak! A total city mouse move. It was pure luck that he wasn't dead. Which was a good thing, because if he died before the wedding, Clara would flat out kill him.

9

"Doc says it was a probably heart attack and we need to get him back to base fast. Didn't say a damn word about how we're supposed to do that." Rico waved at the satellite phone in disgust.

Sonic lay flat on his back on the dining table. It was hard, but Michel forced himself to look at his friend. They were close after five weeks driving on the ice—the whole team was. To see one of their own down was brutal.

But to realize how short time could be was even harder. Just that fast, it could have been him. Maybe not a heart attack, Sonic had a number of issues aside from force-feeding Raisinets, but something else could get him just that fast—like a crevasse.

"Any bright ideas on how to get Sonic to the docs?" Rico asked. "We're still way outside helicopter range to base, even loaded up with extra fuel."

Michel did some quick math in his head. "Two drivers crowd into a cab with no sled load. Figure out how to get Sonic in there too. Then we drive straight through. Bet we could cover the ground in under three days. Even better, at top speed, we could be inside helo range in under twenty-four hours."

"Like the way you think, Frenchy. But we've only got the one ground-penetrating radar. And the tractor would still need to drag a fuel bladder, we don't have any single bladder sleds. We also need to navigate the fall safely, that's a day to do that alone. What else?"

There was a glum silence.

"Well," Michel didn't like being the only one talking up ideas.

But Rico nodded for him to go ahead.

"I spent last summer and a chunk of this spring making the ice runways at MacTown."

"Sonic doesn't have time for us to make a runway."

Michel smiled and pointed out the back door entry to the living quarters. "Don't need to. Have them land an Air National Guard Skibird on the Traverse. We just packed it down with eight tractor loads in two directions. With a little touchup using the plow and another run over the area, that's easily up to spec for those birds. They're tough and we already know the strip is crevasse free."

They were still going to lose a full day by the time all of this was done, but Michel had an idea on that too.

10

————

After cleaning up the section of the SPoT, they staked a two-kilometer stretch with flags every fifty meters.

One of the LC-130 Skibirds flew from McMurdo and wafted down out of the sky to land smooth as could be on the hard-packed snow.

Sonic was aboard in moments. The plane blew a blinding cloud of snow as it turned and raced back aloft. When the blown snow settled to mere white-out, someone in a Big Red parka emerged from the spindrift. He'd know her anywhere, she walked like a sailor who owned the planet.

Six weeks apart and Clara was impossibly even more familiar. All his nerves and worries were gone in that moment.

He walked up and wrapped her in his arms before Sonic's plane was even out of sight.

"Separation makes the heart grow fonder is utter crap, Sailor."

"Why's that, Antoine?"

He laughed. At her. At himself. At the ridiculous places he'd had to go to discover that he had indeed found the woman he loved.

"Answer the question, Jean Baptiste."

"Separation from you is *utter torture.* I get away from you and all I get is FUD—fear, uncertainty, and doubt. You may be a crazy woman, Sailor, but I seem to go far crazier whenever I'm more than about ten feet from you."

She leaned her forehead against his chest for a long moment, "Thank God, Beauregard."

"Why?"

"Because I thought it was just me. That's why I was so nervous when you left. I always made sense to myself until I met you. And now, with you, I make even more sense, but in a whole new way that's so good it's scary."

He couldn't see her face, the bitter wind and the needle-sharp ice forced them to keep their furred hoods up, but this was definitely the right woman for him.

"Come on. I need your help fixing up *your* tractor." He thumped a foot on one of the two boxes that the Skibird had dropped on the snow along with Clara. If they drove the SPoT together, they'd never have to be further apart than their machines.

"What about the wedding?"

He thumped a boot on the second box. "I got that covered."

11

_____

THEY WERE STILL THREE DAYS OUT WHEN IT WAS TIME for the wedding. They'd have a grand party once they were back at McMurdo, but their families were only together for this weekend and they absolutely had to take advantage of it.

The Pole and McMurdo kept New Zealand time, mainly because all of their supply flights originated in Christchurch, New Zealand.

So, the SPoT convoy took a lunchtime-wedding break out on the Ross Ice Shelf. That made for a seven p.m. wedding in Gloucester, Massachusetts.

Priya was at McMurdo on the satellite phone and their families were on another phone. No video conferencing because it was way too expensive via satellite, but that was okay.

Rico had jumped online long enough to become ordained to perform weddings through the Universal

Life Church. And they'd actually bypassed a whole set of problems by not being at McMurdo. Here, in the middle of the Ross Ice Shelf, they were technically in international waters, so there were far fewer legal loopholes for them to jump through.

The team had unhitched the tractors and pulled them into a semicircle to make what Rico called "a churchy space." It also served to block the worst of the wind.

Down on the Ross Ice Shelf, the temperature was again in the twenties, the *positive* twenties. After weeks up on the plateau, it felt incredibly warm and almost comfortable. The driving winds of the Polar Ice Cap had been left behind.

They stood in a vast field of white, only the distant peak of Mount Erebus hinted at land. Above them was a cathedral of crystalline blue as if they were getting married inside a perfect jewel box.

This morning he'd opened the second box that had arrived with Clara. Priya hadn't missed a single thing on his list, right down to the rings from his night table and two bottles of champagne for afterward.

Standing under the Antarctic summer sky, he peeled off his parka. He was wearing his tuxedo, complete with a white bow tie (clip-on because he wasn't crazy). It looked ridiculous with his ski pants and snow boots, but it was his kind of ridiculous.

Clara laughed. "I knew you'd be late for the wedding. But I didn't know you'd be so dashing, Jean

Luc." Then she shed her Big Red parka and he lost his ability to breathe.

She wore the upper half of a wedding dress that wiped out "Sailor" forever.

"You're gorgeous, Clara."

"I'm also turning into a giant goosebump. It's brick out here." The dress was sleeveless, so he slipped his tux jacket over her shoulders and felt morphed into a giant goosebump himself.

A goosebump, but not one with any nerves or doubts. They were impossible with a woman like Clara standing beside him.

Rico held up the two phones: one linking to the maid of honor (and probably half of McMurdo), and the other to their gathered families.

The SPoT crew stood by their tractors like a whole line of men of honor. They'd actually squabbled over who was escorting Clara and who was standing for him. They finally decided that they were all doing both—but they were really on Clara's side.

He could hear them joking about having chosen a particularly deep crevasse if he screwed this up.

Michel glanced at Rico who just shook his head. Why did everyone seem to have the same idea about him?

For all his preparation, the wedding passed in a blur. He was glad one of the guys had offered to video it.

One moment they were freezing together, and the next he was kissing his wife.

In the background he heard cheers from the two phones.

Then he was almost bowled from his feet by the sudden blast of all of the tractor horns firing off at once.

"Oh my God. Please tell me we won't have that for every anniversary." He had to shout to have any chance of being heard. In the brief gaps he could hear the same sounds coming from both phones, blaring horns.

"Every year! It's now mandatory. I love you, Michel Charbonneau."

"Hey, you just used my real name."

She nodded as she dragged on her parka, keeping his jacket. Her hood nodded. "Guess I don't need to keep you at a distance anymore."

And, as usual, Clara was exactly right. With her permanently in his life, he could finally be his true self. The Québécois hero of Antarctica married to the lovely sailor of The Ice.

DRONE (EXCERPT)

IF YOU ENJOYED THAT, YOU'LL LOVE MIRANDA CHASE!

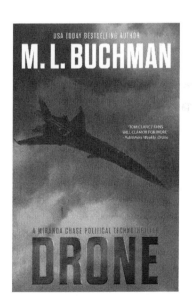

DRONE (EXCERPT)

Flight 630 at 37,000 feet
12 nautical miles north of
Santa Fe, New Mexico, USA

THE FLIGHT ATTENDANT STEPPED UP TO HER SEAT—4E—
which had never been her favorite on a 767-300. At
least the cabin setup was in the familiar 261-seat, 2-
class configuration, currently running at a seventy-
three percent load capacity with a standard crew of ten
and one ride-along FAA inspector in the cockpit jump
seat.

"Excuse me, are you Miranda Chase?"

She nodded.

The attendant made a face that she couldn't
interpret.

A frown? Did that indicate anger?

He turned away before she could consider the possibilities and, without another word, returned to his station at the front of the cabin.

Miranda once again straightened the emergency exit plan that the flight's vibrations kept shifting askew in its pocket.

This flight from yesterday's meeting at LAX to today's DC lunch meeting at the National Transportation Safety Board's headquarters departed so early that she'd decided to spend the night in the airline's executive lounge working on various aviation accident reports. She never slept on a flight and would have to catch up on her sleep tonight.

Miranda felt the shift as the plane turned into a modest five-degree bank to the left. The bright rays of dawn over the New Mexico desert shifted from the left-hand windows to the right side.

At due north, she heard the Rolls-Royce RB211 engines (quite a pleasant high tone compared to the Pratt & Whitney PW4000 that she always found unnerving) ease off ever so slightly, signaling a slow descent. The pilot was transitioning from an eastbound course that would be flown at an odd number of thousands of feet to a westbound one that must be flown at an even number.

The flight attendant then picked up the intercom phone and a loud squawk sounded through the cabin. Most people would be asleep and there were soft complaints and rustling down the length of the aircraft.

"We regret to inform you that there is an emergency on the ground. I repeat, there is nothing wrong with the plane. We are being routed back to Las Vegas, where we will disembark one passenger, refuel, and then continue our flight to DC. Our apologies for the inconvenience."

There were now shouts of complaint all up and down the aisle.

The flight attendant was staring straight at her as he slammed the intercom back into its cradle with significantly greater force than was required to seat it properly.

Oh. It was her they would be disembarking. That meant there was a crash in need of an NTSB investigator—a major one if they were flying back an hour in the wrong direction.

Thankfully, she always had her site kit with her.

For some reason, her seatmate was muttering something foul. Miranda ignored it and began to prepare herself.

Only the crash mattered.

She straightened the exit plan once more. It had shifted the other way with the changing harmonic from the RB211 engines.

———

Chengdu, Central China

AIR FORCE MAJOR WANG FAN EASED BACK ON THE joystick of the final prototype Shenyang J-31 jet—designed exclusively for the People's Liberation Army Air Force. In response, China's newest fighter jet leapt upward like a catapult's missile from the PLAAF base in the flatlands surrounding the towering city of Chengdu.

It felt as he'd just been grasped by Chen Mei-Li. Never had a woman made him feel like such a man.

———

Get Drone *and fly into a whole series of action and danger!*
Available at fine retailers everywhere.
Drone

ABOUT THE AUTHOR

USA Today and Amazon #1 Bestseller M. L. "Matt" Buchman started writing on a flight south from Japan to ride his bicycle across the Australian Outback. Just part of a solo around-the-world trip that ultimately launched his writing career.

From the very beginning, his powerful female heroines insisted on putting character first, *then* a great adventure. He's since written over 60 action-adventure thrillers and military romantic suspense novels. And just for the fun of it: 100 short stories, and a fast-growing pile of read-by-author audiobooks.

Booklist says: "3X Top 10 of the Year." PW says: "Tom Clancy fans open to a strong female lead will clamor for more." His fans say: "I want more now...of everything." That his characters are even more insistent than his fans is a hoot.

As a 30-year project manager with a geophysics degree who has designed and built houses, flown and jumped out of planes, and solo-sailed a 50' ketch, he is awed by what is possible. More at: www.mlbuchman.com.

Other works by M. L. Buchman:

Short Story Series by M. L. Buchman:

SIGN UP FOR M. L. BUCHMAN'S NEWSLETTER TODAY

and receive:
Release News
Free Short Stories
a Free Book

Get your free book today. Do it now.
free-book.mlbuchman.com

Printed in Great Britain
by Amazon

64166023R00050